Dear Parents:

Congratulations! Your child is taking the first steps on an exciting journey. The destination? Independent reading!

STEP INTO READING® will help your child get there. The program offers five steps to reading success. Each step includes fun stories and colorful art or photographs. In addition to original fiction and books with favorite characters, there are Step into Reading Non-Fiction Readers, Phonics Readers and Boxed Sets, Sticker Readers, and Comic Readers—a complete literacy program with something to interest every child.

Learning to Read, Step by Step!

Ready to Read **Preschool–Kindergarten**
• big type and easy words • rhyme and rhythm • picture clues
For children who know the alphabet and are eager to begin reading.

Reading with Help **Preschool–Grade 1**
• basic vocabulary • short sentences • simple stories
For children who recognize familiar words and sound out new words with help.

Reading on Your Own **Grades 1–3**
• engaging characters • easy-to-follow plots • popular topics
For children who are ready to read on their own.

Reading Paragraphs **Grades 2–3**
• challenging vocabulary • short paragraphs • exciting stories
For newly independent readers who read simple sentences with confidence.

Ready for Chapters **Grades 2–4**
• chapters • longer paragraphs • full-color art
For children who want to take the plunge into chapter books but still like colorful pictures.

STEP INTO READING® is designed to give every child a successful reading experience. The grade levels are only guides; children will progress through the steps at their own speed, developing confidence in their reading. The F&P Text Level on the back cover serves as another tool to help you choose the right book for your child.

Remember, a lifetime love of reading starts with a single step!

To Geraldine
and Edgar

Little Critter and the Best Present book, characters, text, and images © 2020 Mercer Mayer

Little Critter, Mercer Mayer's Little Critter, and Mercer Mayer's Little Critter and Logo are registered trademarks of Orchard House Licensing Company.

Step into Reading, Random House, and the Random House colophon are registered trademarks of Penguin Random House LLC.

Visit us on the Web!
StepIntoReading.com
rhcbooks.com
littlecritter.com

Educators and librarians, for a variety of teaching tools, visit us at RHTeachersLibrarians.com

ISBN 978-1-9848-3095-1 (trade) — ISBN 978-0-593-17845-4 (lib. bdg.) — ISBN 978-1-9848-3096-8 (ebook)

Printed in the United States of America
10 9 8 7 6 5 4 3 2 1

This book has been officially leveled by using the F&P Text Level Gradient™ Leveling System.

LITTLE CRITTER®
AND
THE BEST PRESENT

by Mercer Mayer

Random House New York

Today my sister
is five years old!
We will have a party.
It is a surprise!

Dad and I need to
buy a present.

My sister has to
stay home.

Dad and I
drive to the
toy store.

This would
be a good
present.

Or this.

SPECIAL

PET GOO

THROW IT ON A FRIEND

But this is
the best present
for my little sister.

CRITTER PATCH

SHE BURPS
SHE WETS
SHE TALKS
YOU'LL LOVE IT

BUY
ONE
NOW

CRITTER PATCH DOLLS

We go home.

I wrap the present.

I get dressed up.

The doorbell rings.

Surprise!

Everyone is here!

There are

a lot of presents.

There are also
a lot of friends!

We go outside
to play games.

We have a sack race.

We have an
egg race, too.

Then we go inside.

We play more games.

Mom brings out
the birthday cake.

My little sister
makes a wish.
She blows out
all the candles.

Mom cuts the cake.

There is
a lot of cake.

There is a
piece for everyone.

We have
ice cream, too!

Now it is time
to open the presents.

My little sister

opens my present.

"Look at this!"

she says.

She says it is
the best present.
I knew that!